Beatrix Potter's
Beloved Tales

Beatrix Potter's
Beloved Tales

Includes *The Tale of Tom Kitten*,
The Tale of Jemima Puddle-Duck,
The Tale of Mr. Jeremy Fisher,
The Tailor of Gloucester, and
The Tale of Squirrel Nutkin

Beatrix Potter

FOR YOUNG READERS

First published 1902–1908 by Frederick Warne & Co.

First Racehorse for Young Readers Edition 2018.

Racehorse for Young Readers books may be purchased in bulk at special
discounts for sales promotion, corporate gifts, fund-raising, or educa-
tional purposes. Special editions can also be created to specifications.
For details, contact the Special Sales Department, Skyhorse Publishing,
307 West 36th Street, 11th Floor, New York, NY 10018 or
info@skyhorsepublishing.com.

Racehorse for Young Readers™ is a pending trademark of Skyhorse
Publishing, Inc.®, a Delaware corporation.

Visit our website at www.skyhorsepublishing.com.

10 9 8 7 6 5 4 3 2 1

Library of Congress Cataloging-in-Publication Data is available on file.

Cover design by Michael Short
Cover and interior illustrations by Beatrix Potter

ISBN: 978-1-63158-358-2
eISBN: 978-1-63158-359-9

Printed in China

Contents

The Tale of
Tom Kitten

ONCE upon a time there were three little kittens, and their names were Mittens, Tom Kitten, and Moppet.

They had dear little fur coats of their own; and they tumbled about the doorstep and played in the dust.

BUT one day their mother— Mrs. Tabitha Twitchit— expected friends to tea; so she fetched the kittens indoors, to wash and dress them, before the fine company arrived.

FIRST she scrubbed their faces (this one is Moppet).

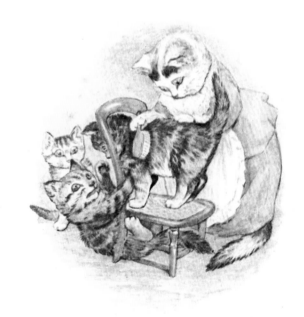

THEN she brushed their fur (this one is Mittens).

THEN she combed their tails and whiskers (this is Tom Kitten).

Tom was very naughty, and he scratched.

MRS. TABITHA dressed Moppet and Mittens in clean pinafores and tuckers; and then she took all sorts of elegant, uncomfortable clothes out of a chest of drawers, in order to dress up her son Thomas.

TOM KITTEN was very fat, and he had grown; several buttons burst off. His mother sewed them on again.

WHEN the three kittens were ready, Mrs. Tabitha unwisely turned them out into the garden, to be out of the way while she made hot buttered toast.

"Now keep your frocks clean, children! You must walk on your hind legs. Keep away from the dirty ash-pit, and from Sally Henny Penny, and from the pig-stye and the Puddle-Ducks."

MOPPET and Mittens walked down the garden path unsteadily. Presently they trod upon their pinafores and fell on their noses.

When they stood up there were several green smears!

"LET us climb up the rockery, and sit on the garden wall," said Moppet.

They turned their pinafores back to front, and went up with a skip and a jump; Moppet's white tucker fell down into the road.

TOM KITTEN was quite unable to jump when walking upon his hind legs in trousers. He came up the rockery by degrees, breaking the ferns, and shedding buttons right and left.

HE was all in pieces when he reached the top of the wall.

Moppet and Mittens tried to pull him together; his hat fell off, and the rest of his buttons burst.

WHILE they were in difficulties, there was a pit pat paddle pat! and the three Puddle-Ducks came along the hard high road, marching one behind the other—and doing the goose step—pit pat paddle pat! pit pat waddle pat!

THEY stopped and stood in a row, and stared up at the kittens. They had very small eyes, and looked surprised.

THEN the two duck-birds, Rebeccah and Jemima Puddle-Duck, picked up the hat and tucker and put them on.

MITTENS laughed so that she fell off the wall. Moppet and Tom descended after her; the pinafores and all the rest of Tom's clothes came off on the way down.

"Come! Mr. Drake Puddle-Duck," said Moppet—"Come and help us to dress him! Come and button up Tom!"

MR. DRAKE PUDDLE-DUCK advanced in a slow, sideways manner, and picked up the various articles.

BUT he put them on *himself!* They fitted him even worse than Tom Kitten.

"It's a very fine morning!" said Mr. Drake Puddle-Duck.

AND he and Jemima and Rebeccah Puddle-Duck set off up the road, keeping step—pit pat, paddle pat! pit pat, waddle pat!

THEN Tabitha Twitchit came down the garden and found her kittens on the wall with no clothes on.

SHE pulled them off the wall, smacked them, and took them back to the house.

"My friends will arrive in a minute, and you are not fit to be seen; I am affronted," said Mrs. Tabitha Twitchit.

SHE sent them upstairs; and I am sorry to say she told her friends that they were in bed with the **measles;** which was not true.

QUITE the contrary; they were not in bed; *not* in the least.

Somehow there were very extraordinary noises overhead; which disturbed the dignity and repose of the tea-party.

A ND I think that some day
I shall have to make
another, larger, book, to tell
you more about Tom Kitten!

AS for the Puddle-Ducks— they went into a pond. The clothes all came off directly, because there were **no** buttons.

AND Mr. Drake Puddle-Duck and Jemima and Rebeccah have been looking for them ever since.

The Tale of
Jemima
Puddle-Duck

WHAT a funny sight it is to see a brood of duck-lings with a hen !
—Listen to the story of Jemima Puddle-duck, who was annoyed because the farmer's wife would not let her hatch her own eggs.

HER sister-in-law, Mrs. Rebeccah Puddle-duck, was perfectly willing to leave the hatching to some one else —"I have not the patience to sit on a nest for twenty-eight days ; and no more have you, Jemima. You would let them go cold; you know you would!"

"I wish to hatch my own eggs; I will hatch them all by myself," quacked Jemima Puddle-duck.

SHE tried to hide her eggs ; but they were always found and carried off.

Jemima Puddle-duck became quite desperate. She determined to make a nest right away from the farm.

SHE set off on a fine spring afternoon along the cart-road that leads over the hill.

She was wearing a shawl and a poke bonnet.

WHEN she reached the top of the hill, she saw a wood in the distance.

She thought that it looked a safe quiet spot.

JEMIMA PUDDLE-DUCK was not much in the habit of flying. She ran downhill a few yards flapping her shawl, and then she jumped off into the air.

SHE flew beautifully when she had got a good start. She skimmed along over the tree-tops until she saw an open place in the middle of the wood where the trees and brushwood had been cleared.

JEMIMA alighted rather heavily, and began to waddle about in search of a convenient dry nesting place. She rather fancied a tree-stump amongst some tall fox-gloves.

But—seated upon the stump, she was startled to find an elegantly dressed gentleman reading a newspaper.

He had black prick ears and sandy coloured whiskers.

"Quack?" said Jemima Puddle-duck, with her head and her bonnet on one side— "Quack?"

THE gentleman raised his eyes above his news-paper and looked curiously at Jemima—

"Madam, have you lost your way?' said he. He had a long bushy tail which he was sitting upon, as the stump was some-what damp.

Jemima thought him mighty civil and handsome. She explained that she had not lost her way, but that she was trying to find a convenient dry nesting-place.

"AH! is that so? indeed!" said the gentleman with sandy whiskers, looking curiously at Jemima. He folded up the newspaper, and put it in his coat tail pocket.

Jemima complained of the superfluous hen.

"Indeed! how interesting! I wish I could meet with that fowl. I would teach it to mind its own business!"

"BUT as to a nest—there is no difficulty: I have a sackful of feathers in my wood-shed. No, my dear madam, you will be in nobody's way. You may sit there as long as you like," said the bushy long-tailed gentleman.

He led the way to a very retired, dismal-looking house amongst the fox-gloves.

It was built of faggots and turf, and there were two broken pails, one on top of another, by way of a chimney.

"THIS is my summer residence; you would not find my earth—my winter house—so convenient," said the hospitable gentleman.

There was a tumble-down shed at the back of the house, made of old soap-boxes. The gentleman opened the door, and showed Jemima in.

THE shed was almost quite full of feathers—it was almost suffocating; but it was comfortable and very soft.

Jemima Puddle-duck was rather surprised to find such a vast quantity of feathers. But it was very comfortable; and she made a nest without any trouble at all.

WHEN she came out, the sandy whiskered gentleman was sitting on a log reading the newspaper—at least he had it spread out, but he was looking over the top of it.

He was so polite, that he seemed almost sorry to let Jemima go home for the night. He promised to take great care of her nest until she came back again next day.

He said he loved eggs and ducklings ; he should be proud to see a fine nestful in his wood-shed.

JEMIMA PUDDLE-DUCK came every afternoon; she laid nine eggs in the nest. They were greeny white and very large. The foxy gentleman admired them immensely. He used to turn them over and count them when Jemima was not there.

At last Jemima told him that she intended to begin to sit next day—"and I will bring a bag of corn with me, so that I need never leave my nest until the eggs are hatched. They might catch cold," said the conscientious Jemima.

"MADAM, I beg you not to trouble yourself with a bag; I will provide oats. But before you commence your tedious sitting, I intend to give you a treat. Let us have a dinner-party all to ourselves!

May I ask you to bring up some herbs from the farm-garden to make a savoury omelette? Sage and thyme, and mint and two onions, and some parsley. I will provide lard for the stuff—lard for the omelette," said the hospitable gentleman with sandy whiskers.

JEMIMA PUDDLE-DUCK was a simpleton : not even the mention of sage and onions made her suspicious.

She went round the farm-garden, nibbling off snippets of all the different sorts of herbs that are used for stuffing roast duck.

AND she waddled into the kitchen, and got two onions out of a basket.

The collie-dog Kep met her coming out, "What are you doing with those onions? Where do you go every after-noon by yourself, Jemima Puddle-duck ?"

Jemima was rather in awe of the collie ; she told him the whole story.

The collie listened, with his wise head on one side ; he grinned when she described the polite gentleman with sandy whiskers.

HE asked several questions about the wood, and about the exact position of the house and shed.

Then he went out, and trotted down the village. He went to look for two fox-hound puppies who were out at walk with the butcher.

JEMIMA PUDDLE-DUCK went up the cart-road for the last time, on a sunny afternoon. She was rather burdened with bunches of herbs and two onions in a bag.

She flew over the wood, and alighted opposite the house of the bushy long-tailed gentleman.

HE was sitting on a log; he sniffed the air, and kept glancing uneasily round the wood. When Jemima alighted he quite jumped.

"Come into the house as soon as you have looked at your eggs. Give me the herbs for the omelette. Be sharp!"

He was rather abrupt. Jemima Puddle-duck had never heard him speak like that.

She felt surprised, and uncomfortable.

WHILE she was inside she heard pattering feet round the back of the shed. Some one with a black nose sniffed at the bottom of the door, and then locked it.

Jemima became much alarmed.

A MOMENT afterwards there were most awful noises — barking, baying, growls and howls, squealing and groans.

And nothing more was ever seen of that foxy-whiskered gentleman.

PRESENTLY Kep opened the door of the shed, and let out Jemima Puddle-duck.

Unfortunately the puppies rushed in and gobbled up all the eggs before he could stop them.

He had a bite on his ear and both of the puppies were limping.

JEMIMA PUDDLE-DUCK was escorted home in tears on account of those eggs.

SHE laid some more in June, and she was permitted to keep them herself: but only four of them hatched.

Jemima Puddle-duck said that it was because of her nerves; but she had always been a bad sitter.

The Tale of
Mr. Jeremy
Fisher

ONCE upon a time there was a frog called Mr. Jeremy Fisher; he lived in a little damp house amongst the buttercups at the edge of a pond.

THE water was all slippy-sloppy in the larder and in the back passage.

But Mr. Jeremy liked getting his feet wet; nobody ever scolded him, and he never caught a cold!

HE was quite pleased when he looked out and saw large drops of rain, splashing in the pond—

" I WILL get some worms and go fishing and catch a dish of minnows for my dinner," said Mr. Jeremy Fisher. "If I catch more than five fish, I will invite my friends Mr. Alderman Ptolemy Tortoise and Sir Isaac Newton. The Alderman, however, eats salad."

M R. JEREMY put on a mackintosh, and a pair of shiny goloshes; he took his rod and basket, and set off with enormous hops to the place where he kept his boat.

THE boat was round and green, and very like the other lily-leaves. It was tied to a water plant in the middle of the pond.

MR. JEREMY took a reed pole, and pushed the boat out into open water. "I know a good place for minnows," said Mr. Jeremy Fisher

MR. JEREMY stuck his pole into the mud and fastened the boat to it.

Then he settled himself cross-legged and arranged his fishing tackle. He had the dearest little red float. His rod was a tough stalk of grass, his line was a fine long white horse-hair, and he tied a little wriggling worm at the end.

THE rain trickled down his back, and for nearly an hour he stared at the float.

"This is getting tiresome, I think I should like some lunch," said Mr. Jeremy Fisher.

HE punted back again amongst the water-plants, and took some lunch out of his basket.

"I will eat a butterfly sandwich, and wait till the shower is over," said Mr. Jeremy Fisher.

A GREAT big water-beetle came up underneath the lily leaf and tweaked the toe of one of his goloshes.

Mr. Jeremy crossed his legs up shorter, out of reach, and went on eating his sandwich.

ONCE or twice something moved about with a rustle and a splash amongst the rushes at the side of the pond.

"I trust that is not a rat," said Mr. Jeremy Fisher; "I think I had better get away from here."

MR. JEREMY shoved the boat out again a little way, and dropped in the bait. There was a bite almost directly; the float gave a tremendous bobbit!

"A minnow! a minnow! I have him by the nose!" cried Mr. Jeremy Fisher, jerking up his rod.

BUT what a horrible surprise! Instead of a smooth fat minnow, Mr. Jeremy landed little Jack Sharp, the stickleback, covered with spines!

THE stickleback floundered about the boat, pricking and snapping until he was quite out of breath. Then he jumped back into the water.

AND a shoal of other little fishes put their heads out, and laughed at Mr. Jeremy Fisher.

AND while Mr. Jeremy sat disconsolately on the edge of his boat—sucking his sore fingers and peering down into the water—a *much* worse thing happened; a really *frightful* thing it would have been, if Mr. Jeremy had not been wearing a mackintosh!

A GREAT big enormous trout came up—ker-pflop-p-p-p! with a splash—and it seized Mr. Jeremy with a snap, Ow! Ow! Ow!"—and then it turned and dived down to the bottom of the pond!

BUT the trout was so dis-pleased with the taste of the mackintosh, that in less than half a minute it spat him out again; and the only thing it swallowed was Mr. Jeremy's goloshes.

MR. JEREMY bounced up to the surface of the water, like a cork and the bubbles out of a soda water bottle; and he swam with all his might to the edge of the pond.

HE scrambled out on the first bank he came to, and he hopped home across the meadow with his mackintosh all in tatters.

"WHAT a mercy that was not a pike!" said Mr. Jeremy Fisher. "I have lost my rod and basket; but it does not much matter, for I am sure I should never have dared to go fishing again!"

HE put some sticking plaster on his fingers, and his friends both came to dinner. He could not offer them fish, but he had something else in his larder.

SIR ISAAC NEWTON wore his black and gold waistcoat.

AND Mr. Alderman Ptolemy Tortoise brought a salad with him in a string bag.

AND instead of a nice dish of minnows they had a roasted grasshopper with lady-bird sauce, which frogs consider a beautiful treat; but *I* think it must have been nasty!

THE END.

The Tailor of
Gloucester

IN the time of swords and periwigs
and full-skirted coats with flowered
lappets—when gentlemen wore ruffles,
and gold-laced waistcoats of paduasoy
and taffeta—there lived a tailor in
Gloucester.

He sat in the window of a little
shop in Westgate Street, cross-legged
on a table from morning till dark.

All day long while the light lasted he
sewed and snippetted, piecing out his
satin, and pompadour, and lutestring;
stuffs had strange names, and were
very expensive in the days of the
Tailor of Gloucester.

But although he sewed fine silk for his neighbours, he himself was very, very poor—a little old man in spectacles, with a pinched face, old crooked fingers, and a suit of threadbare clothes.

He cut his coats without waste, according to his embroidered cloth; they were very small ends and snippets that lay about upon the table—"Too narrow breadths for nought—except waistcoats for mice," said the tailor.

One bitter cold day near Christmas-time the tailor began to make a coat (a coat of cherry-coloured corded silk embroidered with pansies and roses) and a cream-coloured satin waistcoat (trimmed with gauze and green

worsted chenille) for the Mayor of Gloucester.

The tailor worked and worked, and he talked to himself. He measured the silk, and turned it round and round, and trimmed it into shape with his shears; the table was all littered with cherry-coloured snippets.

"No breadth at all, and cut on the cross; it is no breadth at all; tippets for mice and ribbons for mobs! for mice!" said the Tailor of Gloucester.

When the snow-flakes came down against the small leaded window-panes and shut out the light, the tailor had done his day's work; all the silk and satin lay cut out upon the table.

There were twelve pieces for the

coat and four pieces for the waistcoat; and there were pocket-flaps and cuffs and buttons, all in order. For the lining of the coat there was fine yellow taffeta, and for the buttonholes of the waistcoat there was cherry-coloured twist. And everything was ready to sew together in the morning, all measured and sufficient—except that there was wanting just one single skein of cherry-coloured twisted silk.

The tailor came out of his shop at dark, for he did not sleep there at nights; he fastened the window and locked the door, and took away the key. No one lived there at nights but little brown mice, and *they* ran in and out without any keys!

For behind the wooden wainscots of all the old houses in Gloucester, there are little mouse staircases and secret trap-doors; and the mice run from house to house through those long, narrow passages; they can run all over the town without going into the streets.

But the tailor came out of his shop and shuffled home through the snow; he lived quite near by in College Court, next the doorway to College Green. And although it was not a big house, the tailor was so poor he only rented the kitchen.

He lived alone with his cat; it was called Simpkin.

Now all day long while the tailor was out at work, Simpkin kept house

by himself; and he also was fond of the mice, though he gave them no satin for coats!

"Miaw?" said the cat when the tailor opened the door, "miaw?"

The tailor replied: "Simpkin, we shall make our fortune, but I am worn to a ravelling. Take this groat (which is our last fourpence), and, Simpkin, take a china pipkin, buy a penn'orth of bread, a penn'orth of milk, and a penn'orth of sausages. And oh, Simpkin, with the last penny of our fourpence buy me one penn'orth of cherry-coloured silk. But do not lose the last penny of the four-pence, Simpkin, or I am undone and worn to a thread-paper, for I have NO MORE TWIST."

Then Simpkin again said "Miaw!" and took the groat and the pipkin, and went out into the dark.

The tailor was very tired and beginning to be ill. He sat down by the hearth and talked to himself about that wonderful coat.

"I shall make my fortune—to be cut bias—the Mayor of Gloucester is to be married on Christmas Day in the morning, and he hath ordered a coat and an embroidered waistcoat—to be lined with yellow taffeta—and the taffeta sufficeth; there is no more left over in snippets than will serve to make tippets for mice——"

Then the tailor started; for suddenly, interrupting him, from the

dresser at the other side of the kitchen came a number of little noises—

Tip tap, tip tap, tip tap tip!

"Now what can that be?" said the Tailor of Gloucester, jumping up from his chair. The dresser was covered with crockery and pipkins, willow pattern plates, and tea-cups and mugs.

The tailor crossed the kitchen, and stood quite still beside the dresser, listening, and peering through his spectacles. Again from under a tea-cup came those funny little noises—

Tip tap, tip tap, tip tap tip!

"This is very peculiar," said the Tailor of Gloucester, and he lifted up the tea-cup which was upside down.

Out stepped a little live lady mouse, and made a courtesy to the tailor! Then she hopped away down off the dresser, and under the wainscot.

The tailor sat down again by the fire, warming his poor cold hands, and mumbling to himself:—

"The waistcoat is cut out from peach-coloured satin—tambour stitch and rose-buds in beautiful floss silk! Was I wise to entrust my last fourpence to Simpkin? One-and-twenty buttonholes of cherry-coloured twist!"

But all at once, from the dresser, there came other little noises—

Tip tap, tip tap, tip tap tip!

"This is passing extraordinary!" said the Tailor of Gloucester, and

turned over another tea-cup, which was upside down.

Out stepped a little gentleman mouse, and made a bow to the tailor!

And then from all over the dresser came a chorus of little tappings, all sounding together, and answering one another, like watch-beetles in an old worm-eaten window-shutter—

Tip tap, tip tap, tip tap tip!

And out from under tea-cups and from under bowls and basins, stepped other and more little mice, who hopped away down off the dresser and under the wainscot.

The tailor sat down, close over the fire, lamenting: "One-and-twenty buttonholes of cherry-coloured silk!

To be finished by noon of Saturday:
and this is Tuesday evening. Was it
right to let loose those mice, undoubt-
edly the property of Simpkin? Alack,
I am undone, for I have no more
twist!"

The little mice came out again and
listened to the tailor; they took notice
of the pattern of that wonderful coat.
They whispered to one another about
the taffeta lining and about little
mouse tippets.

And then suddenly they all ran
away together down the passage
behind the wainscot, squeaking and
calling to one another as they ran from
house to house; and not one mouse
was left in the tailor's kitchen when

Simpkin came back with the pipkin of milk!

Simpkin opened the door and bounced in, with an angry "G-r-r-miaw!" like a cat that is vexed; for he hated the snow, and there was snow in his ears, and snow in his collar at the back of his neck. He put down the loaf and the sausages upon the dresser, and sniffed.

"Simpkin," said the tailor, "where is my twist?"

But Simpkin set down the pipkin of milk upon the dresser, and looked suspiciously at the tea-cups. He wanted his supper of little fat mouse!

"Simpkin," said the tailor, "where is my TWIST?"

But Simpkin hid a little parcel privately in the tea-pot, and spit and growled at the tailor; and if Simpkin had been able to talk, he would have asked: "Where is my MOUSE?"

"Alack, I am undone!" said the Tailor of Gloucester, and went sadly to bed.

All that night long Simpkin hunted and searched through the kitchen, peeping into cupboards and under the wainscot, and into the tea-pot where he had hidden that twist; but still he found never a mouse!

And whenever the tailor muttered and talked in his sleep, Simpkin said: "Miaw-ger-r-w-s-s-ch!" and made strange, horrid noises, as cats do at night.

For the poor old tailor was very ill with a fever, tossing and turning in his four-post bed; and still in his dreams he mumbled: "No more twist! no more twist!"

All that day he was ill, and the next day, and the next; and what should become of the cherry-coloured coat? In the tailor's shop in Westgate Street the embroidered silk and satin lay cut out upon the table—one-and-twenty buttonholes—and who should come to sew them, when the window was barred, and the door was fast locked?

But that does not hinder the little brown mice; they run in and out without any keys through all the old houses in Gloucester!

Out-of-doors the market folks went trudging through the snow to buy their geese and turkeys, and to bake their Christmas pies; but there would be no Christmas dinner for Simpkin and the poor old tailor of Gloucester.

The tailor lay ill for three days and nights; and then it was Christmas Eve, and very late at night. The moon climbed up over the roofs and chimneys, and looked down over the gateway into College Court. There were no lights in the windows, nor any sound in the houses; all the city of Gloucester was fast asleep under the snow.

And still Simpkin wanted his mice, and mewed as he stood beside the four-post bed.

But it is in the old story that all the beasts can talk in the night between Christmas Eve and Christmas Day in the morning (though there are very few folk that can hear them, or know what it is that they say).

When the Cathedral clock struck twelve there was an answer—like an echo of the chimes — and Simpkin heard it, and came out of the tailor's door, and wandered about in the snow.

From all the roofs and gables and old wooden houses in Gloucester came a thousand merry voices singing the old Christmas rhymes—all the old songs that ever I heard of, and some that I don't know, like Whittington's bells.

First and loudest the cocks cried out: "Dame, get up, and bake your pies!"

"Oh, dilly, dilly, dilly!" sighed Simpkin.

And now in a garret there were lights and sounds of dancing, and cats came from over the way.

"Hey, diddle, diddle, the cat and the fiddle! All the cats in Gloucester—except me," said Simpkin.

Under the wooden eaves the starlings and sparrows sang of Christmas pies; the jackdaws woke up in the Cathedral tower; and although it was the middle of the night the throstles and robins sang; the air was quite full of little twittering tunes.

But it was all rather provoking to poor hungry Simpkin.

Particularly he was vexed with some little shrill voices from behind a wooden lattice. I think that they were bats, because they always have very small voices—especially in a black frost, when they talk in their sleep, like the Tailor of Gloucester.

They said something mysterious that sounded like—

"Buzz, quoth the blue fly; hum, quoth the bee;
Buzz and hum they cry, and so do we!"

and Simpkin went away shaking his ears as if he had a bee in his bonnet.

From the tailor's shop in Westgate came a glow of light; and when Simpkin crept up to peep in at the window

it was full of candles. There was a snippeting of scissors, and snappeting of thread; and little mouse voices sang loudly and gaily:

"Four-and-twenty tailors
Went to catch a snail,
The best man amongst them
Durst not touch her tail;
She put out her horns
Like a little kyloe cow.
Run, tailors, run! or she'll have you all e'en now!"

Then without a pause the little mouse voices went on again:

"Sieve my lady's oatmeal,
Grind my lady's flour,
Put it in a chestnut,
Let it stand an hour——"

"Mew! Mew!" interrupted Simpkin, and he scratched at the door.

But the key was under the tailor's pillow; he could not get in.

The little mice only laughed, and tried another tune—

"Three little mice sat down to spin,
Pussy passed by and she peeped in.
What are you at, my fine little men?
Making coats for gentlemen.
Shall I come in and cut off your threads?
Oh, no, Miss Pussy, you'd bite off our heads!"

"Mew! Mew!" cried Simpkin.

"Hey diddle dinketty!" answered the little mice—

"Hey diddle dinketty, poppetty pet!
The merchants of London they wear scarlet;
Silk in the collar, and gold in the hem,
So merrily march the merchantmen!"

They clicked their thimbles to mark the time, but none of the songs pleased

Simpkin; he sniffed and mewed at the door of the shop.

"And then I bought
A pipkin and a popkin,
A slipkin and a slopkin,
All for one farthing——

and upon the kitchen dresser!" added the rude little mice.

"Mew! scratch! scratch!" scuffled Simpkin on the window-sill; while the little mice inside sprang to their feet, and all began to shout at once in little twittering voices: "No more twist! No more twist!" And they barred up the window-shutters and shut out Simpkin.

But still through the nicks in the shutters he could hear the click of

thimbles, and little mouse voices singing:

"No more twist! No more twist!"

Simpkin came away from the shop and went home considering in his mind. He found the poor old tailor without fever, sleeping peacefully.

Then Simpkin went on tip-toe and took a little parcel of silk out of the tea-pot; and looked at it in the moonlight; and he felt quite ashamed of his badness compared with those good little mice!

When the tailor awoke in the morning, the first thing which he saw, upon the patchwork quilt, was a skein of cherry-coloured twisted silk, and beside his bed stood the repentant Simpkin!

"Alack, I am worn to a ravelling," said the tailor of Gloucester, "but I have my twist!"

The sun was shining on the snow when the tailor got up and dressed, and came out into the street with Simpkin running before him.

The starlings whistled on the chimney stacks, and the throstles and robins sang—but they sang their own little noises, not the words they had sung in the night.

"Alack," said the tailor, "I have my twist; but no more strength—nor time —than will serve to make me one single buttonhole; for this is Christmas Day in the Morning! The Mayor of Gloucester shall be married by noon

—and where is his cherry-coloured coat?"

He unlocked the door of the little shop in Westgate Street, and Simpkin ran in, like a cat that expects something.

But there was no one there! Not even one little brown mouse!

The boards were swept and clean; the little ends of thread and the little silk snippets were all tidied away, and gone from off the floor.

But upon the table—oh joy! the tailor gave a shout—there, where he had left plain cuttings of silk—there lay the most beautifullest coat and embroidered satin waistcoat that ever were worn by a Mayor of Gloucester!

There were roses and pansies upon the facings of the coat; and the waistcoat was worked with poppies and corn-flowers.

Everything was finished except just one single cherry-coloured buttonhole, and where that buttonhole was wanting there was pinned a scrap of paper with these words—in little teeny weeny writing—

NO MORE TWIST.

And from then began the luck of the Tailor of Gloucester; he grew quite stout, and he grew quite rich.

He made the most wonderful waist-coats for all the rich merchants of Gloucester, and for all the fine gentle-men of the country round.

Never were seen such ruffles, or such embroidered cuffs and lappets! But his buttonholes were the greatest triumph of it all.

The stitches of those buttonholes were so neat—*so* neat—I wonder how they could be stitched by an old man in spectacles, with crooked old fingers, and a tailor's thimble.

The stitches of those buttonholes were so small—*so* small—they looked as if they had been made by little mice!

THE END

The Tale of
Squirrel Nutkin

THIS is a Tale about a tail— a tail that belonged to a little red squirrel, and his name was Nutkin.

He had a brother called Twinkleberry, and a great many cousins; they lived in a wood at the edge of a lake.

IN the middle of the lake there is an island covered with trees and nut bushes; and amongst those trees stands a hollow oak-tree, which is the house of an owl who is called Old Brown.

ONE autumn when the nuts were ripe, and the leaves on the hazel bushes were golden and green—Nutkin and Twinkleberry and all the other little squirrels came out of the wood, and down to the edge of the lake.

THEY made little rafts out of twigs, and they paddled away over the water to Owl Island to gather nuts.

Each squirrel had a little sack and a large oar, and spread out his tail for a sail.

THEY also took with them an offering of three fat mice as a present for Old Brown, and put them down upon his door-step.

Then Twinkleberry and the other little squirrels each made a low bow, and said politely—

"Old Mr. Brown, will you favor us with permission to gather nuts upon your island?"

BUT Nutkin was excessively impertinent in his manners. He bobbed up and down like a little red *cherry*, singing—

"Riddle me, riddle me, rot-tot-tote!
  A little wee man in a red, red coat!
  A staff in his hand, and a stone in his
      throat;
  If you'll tell me this riddle, I'll give you a
      groat."

Now this riddle is as old as the hills; Mr. Brown paid no attention whatever to Nutkin.

He shut his eyes obstinately and went to sleep.

THE squirrels filled their little sacks with nuts, and sailed away home in the evening.

BUT next morning they all came back again to Owl Island; and Twinkleberry and the others brought a fine fat mole, and laid it on the stone in front of Old Brown's doorway, and said—

"Mr. Brown, will you favor us with your gracious permission to gather some more nuts?"

BUT Nutkin, who had no respect, began to dance up and down, tickling old Mr. Brown with a *nettle* and singing—

> "Old Mr. B! Riddle-me-ree!
> Hitty Pitty within the wall,
> Hitty Pitty without the wall;
> If you touch Hitty Pitty,
> Hitty Pitty will bite you!"

Mr. Brown woke up suddenly and carried the mole into his house.

HE shut the door in Nutkin's face. Presently a little thread of blue *smoke* from a wood fire came up from the top of the tree, and Nutkin peeped through the key-hole and sang—

"A house full, a hole full!
And you cannot gather a bowl-full!"

THE squirrels searched for nuts all over the island and filled their little sacks.

But Nutkin gathered oak-apples—yellow and scarlet—-and sat upon a beech-stump playing marbles, and watching the door of Old Mr. Brown.

ON the third day the squirrels got up very early and went fishing; they caught seven fat minnows as a present for Old Brown.

They paddled over the lake and landed under a crooked chestnut-tree on Owl Island.

TWINKLEBERRY and six other little squirrels each carried a fat minnow; but Nutkin, who had no nice manners, brought no present at all. He ran in front, singing—

"The man in the wilderness said to me,
  'How many strawberries grow in the sea?'
  I answered him as I thought good—
  'As many red herrings as grow in the
    wood.'"

But Old Mr. Brown took no interest in riddles—not even when the answer was provided for him.

ON the fourth day the squirrels brought a present of six fat beetles, which were as good as plums in *plum-pudding* for Old Brown. Each beetle was wrapped up carefully in a dock-leaf, fastened with a pine-needle pin.

But Nutkin sang as rudely as ever—

"Old Mr. B! riddle-me-ree!
  Flour of England, fruit of Spain,
  Met together in a shower of rain;
  Put in a bag tied round with a string,
  If you'll tell me this riddle I'll give you a
    ring!"

Which was ridiculous of Nutkin, because he had not got any ring to give to Old Brown.

THE other squirrels hunted up and down the nut bushes; but Nutkin gathered robin's pin-cushions off a briar bush, and stuck them full of pine-needle pins.

ON the fifth day the squirrels brought a present of wild honey; it was so sweet and sticky that they licked their fingers as they put it down upon the stone. They had stolen it out of a bumble *bees*' nest on the tippitty top of the hill.

But Nutkin skipped up and down, singing—

"Hum-a-bum! buzz! buzz! Hum-a-bum buzz!
 As I went over Tipple-tine
 I met a flock of bonny swine;
Some yellow-nacked, some yellow backed!
 They were the very bonniest swine
 That e'er went over Tipple-tine."

OLD Mr. Brown turned up
his eyes in disgust at the
impertinence of Nutkin.
But he ate up the honey!

THE squirrels filled their little sacks with nuts.

But Nutkin sat upon a big flat rock, and played ninepins with a crab apple and green fir-cones.

ON the sixth day, which was Saturday, the squirrels came again for the last time; they brought a new laid *egg* in a little rush basket as a last parting present for Old Brown.

But Nutkin ran in front laughing, and shouting—

"Humpty Dumpty lies in the beck,
  With a white counterpane round his neck,
  Forty doctors and forty wrights,
  Cannot put Humpty Dumpty to rights!"

NOW Old Mr. Brown took an interest in eggs; he opened one eye and shut it again. But still he did not speak.

NUTKIN became more and more impertinent—

"Old Mr. B! Old Mr. B!
Hickamore, Hackamore, on the King's
          kitchen door;
All the King's horses, and all the
          King's men,
Couldn't drive Hickamore, Hackamore,
Off the King's kitchen door."

Nutkin danced up and down like a *sunbeam*, but still Old Brown said nothing at all.

NUTKIN began again—

"Arthur O'Bower has broken his band,
  He comes roaring up the land!
  The King of Scots with all his power,
  Cannot turn Arthur of the Bower!"

Nutkin made a whirring noise to sound like the *wind*, and he took a running jump right onto the head of Old Brown! . . . .

Then all at once there was a flutterment and a scufflement and a loud "Squeak!"

The other squirrels scuttered away into the bushes.

WHEN they came back very cautiously peeping round the tree—there was Old Brown sitting on his door-step, quite still, with his eyes closed, as if nothing had happened.

*   *   *   *   *   *

But Nutkin was in his waist-coat pocket!

THIS looks like the end of the story; but it isn't.

OLD BROWN carried Nutkin into his house, and held him up by the tail, intending to skin him; but Nutkin pulled so very hard that his tail broke in two, and he dashed up the staircase and escaped out of the attic window.

AND to this day if you meet Nutkin up a tree and ask him a riddle, he will throw sticks at you and stamp his feet and scold, and shout—

"C u c k - cuck-cuck-cur-r-r- cuck-k-k!"

THE END.